Collins

HOLE IN THE ROAD

ANNE FINE

1
"OFF TO AUSTRALIA?"

You want to know how it happened? The answer is – the way it always does. I have a really good idea. And it turns into trouble.

It was a bad start to the day because I had to catch up with revision homework for Mrs Miller.

"It must be done by Monday, Will," she'd said.

Mum had let my mate Eddie in as usual that morning, if only because he'd told her he had to do revision too. But it was very boring. So, when we suddenly heard the whine of a drill start up in the next street, I said that I was sneaking out to take a look.

2

And Eddie came as well because he is (as Mrs Miller puts it) "far too easy to lead into trouble, Will". And he is, too.

I've been best friends with Eddie ever since we met in nursery school when we were three. Mum says that I was standing on the spotted rug, holding my breath out of sheer temper. Eddie came in with his dad and watched, amazed, as my face went more and more blue.

Mum says that Eddie spent the whole of that first morning taking giant breaths and holding them as long as he could, hoping his own face would turn as wonderfully blue as mine.

We've stuck together ever since, in one school after another. Some of the teachers try to separate us. "Go and sit over there, Will." Or, "Choose someone else to work with today, please, Eddie." But it's never for long because I'm good at helping Eddie with his work. And he spends most of his weekends at my house, if I'm not over with him at his.

So off we went to find out where the noise was coming from. It was across the road, beside the park. Four men were working on a hole in the road. We stood there for a while, Eddie and me, happily watching the hole slowly getting deeper and deeper.

Two of the men had spades. The one who used the drill was taking a bit of a break. And the last one was inspecting his phone.

"Off to Australia?" asked Eddie.

Okay, maybe it wasn't the best joke ever. And they had probably heard it before. Eight million times. But there was no need for all four of them to roll their eyes.

It didn't bother Eddie. I can't say he's the most sensitive soul around. But I was a little embarrassed.

Just at that moment, I saw Eddie's dad ambling towards us. "Hi, lads," he said as he drew close. "I see you're busy watching other people do something useful, as usual."

He stopped and peered into the hole. "Off to Australia?" he asked.

One of the workmen rolled his eyes again, but the other three did make a stab at chuckling politely. (Eddie's dad is rather big. You wouldn't want to get on the wrong side of him.)

6

Eddie's dad turned to us and said, "Hey, lads. You see the muscles on those arms? That's honest work for you. And not one of these guys is much older than you!"

Eddie was stung. "They are *way* older than me and Will!"

"Nonsense!" his dad said. "You should take a look at some of the students in the Charity Week parade heading for Tanner Street right now. They can't be more than a couple of years older than you two. And you could swap those lads for the four working in this hole, and never notice the difference."

And after one last look at what the men were doing, Eddie's dad strolled off along the street, merrily whistling.

2

MY BRILLIANT IDEA

As soon as his dad was gone, Eddie asked, "Will, what's Charity Week?"

I shrugged. "I think it's mostly students doing weird things like dressing up as aliens or dyeing their hair green. My mum says last year a load of them got themselves up as zombies and lurched around outside her supermarket. There was a picture in the local paper. But in the end the manager ordered them away because they kept on climbing in the shopping trolleys."

"Wow!" Eddie said. "I'd love to go round acting like a zombie for a day."

"They had amazing make-up – all torn-out hair and blood and scars and stuff. And other students pretended to be victims and ran away from them. I wish I'd been there."

"But what's it all for?"

"To raise money. Last year it all went to the local hospital. And on the posters it says that this year all the money's going to help build the new play park."

"Oh, right." Eddie leaned forward again and took another look into the hole. "My dad's right. They do look young, don't they?"

I studied each of them in turn. One was just starting to grow a beard. He hadn't got too far – a few pale, floaty wisps, that's all. One looked no older than Eddie's brother, who only left school last year. The third one had a chubby face, so it was difficult to tell how old he was.

The last workman was facing the other way and kept his head down. But he was short and wiry, and from the back he looked as if he could have been anything from fifteen to twenty-five.

Suddenly, Eddie dug an elbow in my side. "Watch out," he warned. "Look who's on her way down here."

He pointed up the street. It was my mum.

"We're meant to be doing revision," he reminded me. "Do you suppose she's checking up on us?"

"She might be," I admitted. "Though she's probably just on her way home from work."

"But it's much quicker to get to your house down Tanner Street. Why's she coming this way?"

I sighed. "Don't think she won't take time out from her busy life to tell us – in the greatest detail."

"Too late to hide?"

It was. My mum had spotted us. "What are you boys doing, loafing around here? You're supposed to be doing your homework!"

She handed one giant bag of food shopping to Eddie and one to me. "Since you're not doing anything useful, you can carry these home for me."

Mine weighed a ton. It must have been full of bricks. And poor old Eddie's looked even heavier, as if she'd filled it with a heap of weights she'd stolen from some gym.

We trailed along behind her. "Why did you come this way?" I asked, wondering why we'd been unlucky enough to meet her.

"Tanner Street's all bunged up," she said. "Something to do with students and Charity Week."

Then she scowled. "Some baby-faced police officer stopped me cutting across the parade. I told him the bags were heavy and I didn't want to go the long way round, but he still wouldn't budge."

Reaching our door, she tugged out her key. "I don't know what the world is coming to when someone as young as him has the bare-faced cheek to tell someone my age which roads she can and can't cross."

She kept up the grumbling as we dumped her shopping bags on the table. "Policeman? I'll swear the lad can't have been a day older than either of you two. Why, he looked even younger than most of the students in the parade!"

That's when I hatched my *brilliant* idea.

3

WHO IS THE BRAINS HERE?

It took a bit of time to get the plan straight in Eddie's brain. (He's not that bright.) He kept on asking questions.

"But surely ... ?"

"But won't ... ?"

"But if ... ?"

"But when ... ?"

"But how ... ?"

"Listen," I told him, as we followed the noise of the brass band and the cheering back towards Tanner Street. "Just do exactly what I say and it'll work. It'll be a good laugh."

Eddie put on his Baffled Man look. "I still don't get it, Will."

"Eddie! Who is the brains here? Me or you? Just trust me and follow my orders."

Eddie gave up. "All right." By then, we'd caught up with the Charity Week parade. Crowds lined both sides of the road.

We stood and watched as the brass band went past, playing a march. After that came the floats.

The first was an open lorry that had been made to look like an underwater palace with a sea king and mermaids in bikini tops. Long strings of seaweed trailed around the float, and down the sides. To one side sat a giant octopus, waving its arms.

Eddie took time to count them. "Six, seven, eight! Mistake!"

"Why?" I asked.

"An octopus only has six legs."

"That's insects," I told him.

The next float was a hair salon with a line of chairs. The students on them all had crazy hair in even crazier colours. And some had so much glitter on the top that it was spilling around them.

"You'd look good like that," I said to Eddie.

He grinned. "Can you imagine Mrs Miller's face?"

Running along beside the floats were students shaking buckets of money at the passers-by. Eddie never has any money. But I dipped in my pocket and found a couple of coins, so I gave those.

We worked our way along the street. Every now and again we saw a police officer telling people to get back on the pavements, so that they didn't get run over by the giant lorries and tractors pulling the floats.

My mum was quite right. One of the officers did look very young indeed – almost a boy. If you had made him stand beside the boys in the top year group in our school, lots of them would have looked older.

Next round the corner came a trailer with five pretty milkmaids blowing kisses, and five massive cardboard cows.

"Those cows are the same shape as you, Will!" Eddie teased.

After that came a boxing ring with two men in great big padded fat suits pretending to fight one another.

"See those?" I teased him back. "Same shape as you."

Then came the clowns and acrobats. It was a good parade and took a bit of time to pass. I kept trying to drag Eddie away so we could get on with My Plan. But he was enjoying it too much, especially the mermaids and milkmaids.

4

FINGERS CROSSED

"Right," Eddie said, as we hurried back across the park towards the hole in the road. "Tell me again. What do I have to say?"

I laid it on him for the millionth time. He muttered the little speech over and over, then stopped at the park gate to practise his "innocent" face – the one he turns on his mum and Mrs Miller each time they tell him off. "Think it'll work?"

"Your innocent face? I doubt it. After all, it never works on your mum or Mrs Miller."

He sighed. "You never know. The workmen might be dumber than they are."

"Fingers crossed," I said, and I hopped over the wall, out of sight. "Good luck!"

Taking a deep breath, Eddie set off along the pavement in plain view. Behind the wall, I crept along beside him, still out of sight, until I reached a giant clump of bushes. It was quite near the hole in the road, so I could stand behind it and raise my head to watch without being noticed.

I saw Eddie grin at the workmen in his friendliest way, and wave at the man with the drill to make him switch it off.

The drill whined to a halt.

Then, "Hey!" said Eddie. "I just wanted to tell you all that you're missing the parade!" He pointed. "It's only just gone round that corner. If you hurry you can still catch it."

The workmen stared blankly at him, as if he was a right plonker. Wispy Beard said scornfully to his mates, "I don't suppose the poor lad's ever heard of the word '*work*'."

"Or getting a job done," said Chubby Face.

"Or earning your pay," said the one who looked no older than Eddie's brother.

"Or not just knocking off the moment you feel like a break," the short and wiry one growled at his boots.

Eddie pretended that he didn't understand the insults. "You ought to go," he insisted. "It's really funny, because some of the students have dressed up as police officers, and they keep going round ordering busy people to stop work."

None of the workmen bothered to say a word.

Eddie kept on as if he hadn't noticed. "And because their uniforms look exactly right," he continued, "people believe them and knock off what they're doing."

He waved a hand at the workmen. "Well," he said, "all I'm saying is, you're missing a really good parade."

"We'll live," said Chubby Face, sourly.

And we heard nothing else because the drill was turned back on as Eddie drifted away.

5

A REALLY IMPORTANT MESSAGE

"Job done," said Eddie proudly, as soon as he was near enough to make himself heard over the noise of the drill. "Now let's see how you get on with your half of the plan."

Now that we'd come so close to me doing my bit, the idea didn't seem so brilliant. But Eddie had bravely played his part. So, even though I was having serious second thoughts, I didn't think that I should let him down.

Back we went, not past the workmen but the other way down Tanner Street, until we caught up with the end of the parade.

I searched the street for the baby-faced policeman, and found him chatting to some bloke with a toddler so fast asleep in its stroller that even the brass band hadn't woken it.

"Maybe we ought to think again," I said to Eddie. (After all, a police officer is a police officer, even if he does look so young you reckon his mum might order him up to bed at half past ten.)

But Eddie dug his fist in my back to push me closer. "Go on!"

Telling a massive lie to someone in uniform is not the smartest idea. So, coming to my senses, I changed my mind about the whole great plan.

"Eddie ... "

But he'd already stepped forward. "Officer!"

Pointing at me, he said, "He's got a message for you and it's really important."

I honestly can't understand what happened next. I think I must have panicked. I opened my mouth, and what I *meant* to say was, "Don't listen to my friend here, Officer. He's talking *rubbish*. I don't have any message."

But what came out was what we'd practised twenty times behind the wall when I still thought it was a brilliant idea.

I said, "Officer, I think you ought to know that in the next street there are some Charity Week students with a road drill, digging a giant great hole in the road."

The officer didn't believe me, I could tell. He gave me a tired look. "Oh, very likely."

I didn't add the next bit. *Eddie* did. He is an *idiot* sometimes.

"No, *really*. The hole's enormous! Go and see!"

6

THAT'S WHEN THE TROUBLE STARTED

You can imagine how things panned out after that.

The police officer ran off in the direction of the workmen and the hole, and I could see him talking into his radio.

I followed Eddie as he crept along behind the wall. (I didn't think that I could leave someone so *stupid* out on the streets by himself.)

We reached the bushes and raised our heads just high enough to peep over.

The police officer had arrived as well, and he was saying, very firmly indeed, "You lads in there. You stop right now! Stop digging that hole at once!"

But Eddie had done his own half of our double act so well that the workmen ignored him.

"You heard me!" said the officer. "Stop digging! That's an *order*."

I saw the workmen roll their eyes at one another, as they kept working and pretended they were deaf.

"This instant! Now! Get out of this hole at once!"

Chubby Face looked up and said, "Run away, lad. You really think that you can fool us into believing that's a real uniform?"

"I can assure you ... "

But the policeman didn't get the chance
to say another word because the workman
interrupted him.

"Push off. Right now. We know you're not a
real officer. You're just dressed up for your parade.
So go and find someone else to annoy. Some of us
have work to do."

And then his mate turned on the drill.

That's when the trouble really started. I saw the
policeman mouth helplessly into the giant drilling
noise, then walk away.

"Shame!" Eddie sighed. "After all that effort we
put into learning our lines, the row didn't last very
long, did it?"

How wrong can your best mate be? Because as soon as the police officer had walked far enough away from the hole in the road to make himself heard, he used his radio again.

To call for back up.

I suppose it was pure chance that the next officer to arrive looked almost as young as him.

She started up the same way he had. "Right, you! Put down that drill! The rest of you, stop digging at once!"

The workmen looked up wearily. "Oh, not *again*!"

"Look, Miss! Joke over."

"Leave us to get on with our work."

"Go and bother someone else."

On went the drill again, so Eddie and I missed some of the next bit. But from the mouthing and the angry faces, I reckoned there was quite a fierce argument brewing. Then off went the drill.

We caught the flavour, and yes, you could say it was getting nastier.

" – flaming idiots!"

" – hindering a police officer in the course of her duty!"

" – nothing better to do than dress up and swan about bothering people who are trying to do an honest day's work!"

" – warn you that you are risking arrest!"

" – just go back to your stupid college and see if you can grow a brain!"

If anything, things started to get worse ...

" – causing criminal damage!"

" – good mind to get out of this hole and rearrange your face!"

" – going to have to pay for this mess in the road!"

" – losing my patience now!"

I reckon they could have gone on at each other all day. But that's when we heard the sirens, and a sleek shiny squad car with a blue flashing light squealed round the corner and came scorching to a halt.

Four more uniformed officers got out and loomed over the hole.

The workmen stared. Everyone knows you can't rent pretend squad cars. Or police sirens. Or blue flashing lights. And none of the officers who'd arrived looked very young. In fact, three of the four had greying hair, and one looked positively *ancient*.

These officers certainly didn't look like Charity Week students.

The workmen stared some more. Then they looked sheepishly at one another. And all six police officers looked back at them.

There was the most uneasy silence.

I was glad to go.

1

"DO YOU RECKON WE'RE OK NOW?"

That's when we legged it, really fast, along behind the wall. We kept our heads well down. We ran the whole way over the park to the bandstand, so nobody would guess we lived so close to where the trouble was.

We waited by the bandstand a few more minutes. And then we crept back, and across the road to my house, hoping that we'd be safe.

Mum offered us a snack as we rushed through the kitchen.

"No time for that!" I shouted back, as we thudded up the stairs.

We were both panting from the run. I threw myself on my bed and Eddie lay flat out on my old rug.

It was a while before I had enough breath to speak.

"Maybe that wasn't the smartest idea I ever had," I said.

"I don't think it was," agreed Eddie. "Though it was a laugh at the time. Do you reckon we're OK now?"

I forced myself to get up so that I could peer out of the window. "There's no one out there."

"*Yet* ..." said Eddie gloomily.

We waited a little longer, with our ears pinned back, hoping not to hear any knocking on the front door, and police officers asking Mum where we had been half an hour before.

Then, as soon as we felt safe, I went downstairs and made the snack that Mum had offered us when we came in.

In between mouthfuls, Eddie said, "That was a good laugh, Will. I really enjoyed it. What are we going to do next?"

"Nothing," I said, and I pulled out the homework book that Mrs Miller had been going on about for so long, nagging me over and over.

"Will, you do realise there's an exam quite soon, don't you?" she'd kept on saying. "So when am I finally going to see this homework book of yours brought up to date?"

I had decided it would be today. Digging that hole had looked like really hard work to me. I didn't fancy that. Mucking about on floats looked so much easier.

So I went back to my exam revision.

Eddie did moan a bit. But I ignored him. And after about half an hour of picking polystyrene beads out of my bean bag, Eddie got bored enough to start on his revision too.

See? Easy to lead. (I told you.)

All in all, both of us reckoned it had been a pretty good day.

Until we heard the sirens coming around the corner.

Into our street ...

Reader challenge

Word hunt

1 On page 8, find an adjective that means "a bit annoyed".

2 On page 20, find a verb that means "smiled widely".

3 On page 42, find a word that means "about to start" or "on the way".

Story sense

4 How does Will describe Charity Week? (page 9)

5 What sorts of things did the lads see on the parade floats? (pages 19–23)

6 Why did Eddie tell the workmen that the police officers were really students dressed up? (page 27)

7 Why did Will think Eddie was so stupid? (page 36)

8 How do you think the workmen felt when they realised the police officers were real? Give reasons. (pages 44–45)

Your views

9 Do you think Will and Eddie were right to go through with the plan? Give reasons.

10 Why do you think the author ended the story with the police sirens coming into Will's street?

Spell it

With a partner, look at these words and then cover them up:

- politely
- firmly
- helplessly

Take it in turns for one of you to read the words aloud. The other person has to try and spell each word. Check your answers, then swap over.

Try it

With a partner, imagine you are Will and Eddie and have just heard the police sirens coming into the street. Think about what you would do and say. Role-play the situation.

William Collins's dream of knowledge for all began with the publication of his first book in 1819. A self-educated mill worker, he not only enriched millions of lives, but also founded a flourishing publishing house. Today, staying true to this spirit, Collins books are packed with inspiration, innovation and practical expertise. They place you at the centre of a world of possibility and give you exactly what you need to explore it.

Collins. Freedom to teach.

Published by Collins Education
An imprint of HarperCollins*Publishers*
77-85 Fulham Palace Road
Hammersmith
London
W6 8JB

Browse the complete Collins Education catalogue at **www.collins.co.uk**

Text © Anne Fine 2014
Illustrations by Paul Fisher © HarperCollins*Publishers* 2014

Series consultants: Alan Gibbons and Natalie Packer

10 9 8 7 6 5 4 3 2 1
ISBN 978-0-00-746481-4

British Library Cataloguing in Publication Data.
A catalogue record for this publication is available from the British Library.

Commissioned by Catherine Martin
Edited by Sue Chapple
Project-managed by Lucy Hobbs and Caroline Green
Illustration management by Tim Satterthwaite
Proofread by Hugh Hillyard-Parker
Typeset by Jouve India, Ltd
Production by Emma Roberts
Printed and bound in China by South China Printing Co.
Cover design by Paul Manning

Acknowledgements

The publishers would like to thank the students and teachers of the following schools for their help in trialling the *Read On* series:

Parkview School, London
Ralph Thoresby School, Leeds
Southfields Academy, London
Wellacre Academy, Manchester
Ormiston Six Villages Academy, Chichester